The Boy
and his Friend
the Blizzard

Illustrations by BRIAN WILDSMITH

GREGORY MARTON

THE

AND HIS

THE

HARPER & ROW

BOY

FRIEND

BLIZZARD

Publishers · New York and Evanston

F
Mar
c.2

© 1962 BY G. B. MARTON

ILLUSTRATIONS © 1962 BY
JONATHAN CAPE LTD

FIRST EDITION

LIBRARY OF CONGRESS CATALOG CARD NUMBER: 62-19603

To my wife,
Elizabeth

HE was a young boy, mere thirteen, and he had gone three days now without having a meal. There was nothing unusual about that, and the boy carried his misfortune with no loss of true pride.

Everything about him was young and fragile except his eyes, which looked old and defeated. When he walked he moved with the swiftness of a forest beast; when cornered he became rough and harsh-spoken.

People made fun of the boy (on account of his oversize boots which surpassed his feet in bulk), and he was not angry. Others looked at him with pity and were sad. Yet very few of the kinder people talked to him, asking polite, meaningless questions which he hated and never answered.

I walked these streets for three days and did nothing, he thought. Today I'll try this state-owned restaurant. Its manager is a small, fat man. I like fat people with their big, happy voices.

But the fat man wasn't in a happy mood.

'What do you want?' he whispered angrily.

'Something to eat,' the boy said quietly.

'Have you money?'

9

'No.'

'Ha! So you are one of those fugitives?'

The boy did not know what fugitive meant so he replied sternly:

'I'm hungry.'

'What's it to me?'

'Nothing,' the boy said.

The fat man picked up a plate from the counter.

'Scram,' he whispered, 'or I'll crown you with this. I remember throwing you out the day before yesterday.'

'Today I am hungrier.'

'Ah, drop dead,' the fat man murmured and put back the plate.

'I would,' the boy said simply. 'But I want to live till Christmas.'

'What for? Will Saint Nicholas bring you something?'

'Perhaps,' the boy replied. He looked up at the ceiling, then to the fat man. 'There is something I can give you.'

'Money?'

'This.'

And he dropped a very small medal on the counter.

'What's this?' the fat man howled.

'Saint Anthony.'

'A fetish, eh?'

'A piece of silver,' the boy remarked obligingly. 'Money.'

'I can't take that sort of money, you know.'

'I know,' the boy said happily, and put the medal back into his pocket. He was sure he had the fat man, who was a weak bargainer, hiding behind a tirade of vehement words.

'Send it to that table over there.' He smiled with his sad, brown eyes, then added for good measure, 'Saint Anthony will bless you for it.'

'The devil take you and your Anthony.'

But the boy had not heard him. He felt confident, for he knew that he could trick anyone if he wanted to badly enough. He held a bundle of blanket tightly under his right arm and walked to a table by the door. It pays to sit near a door. One sees and one can make a quick getaway.

There will be bad weather in two or three days, he thought, but not tomorrow. Get a good feed now and some sleep if possible. Tomorrow you must be smart. Tomorrow you must make it.

Before the supper arrived he opened the folds of

the blanket, spreading it out on the table with great care and ceremony. In it there was a battered old exercise book with a great red star adorning its cover. Some time ago the boy had thought of removing the big star—cutting it out completely. But that would have weakened the stiffness of the book.

He was very fond of the book. He carried in it an old tinted photograph of his mother who died two years ago. On her death-bed she had made him promise to write his sorrows upon the rough pages which were ruled with faint blue lines. 'I'll come by night, every night, and shall read it. But write only when you feel very lonely.'

The boy felt lonely all the time. But the book held only forty pages, and the boy kept the greater part of his sadness unwritten. Besides, two weeks ago, he bartered his pen for a piece of hard *kolbasz* which is what people call sausage in Hungarian.

He always thought of his mother as he had last seen her: dead and rigid. Two copper coins were resting on her eyes, in order to keep the eyelids shut. In her hands she held a wooden cross which was not hers but was placed there by the nuns who were allowed to work in hospitals on account of the shortage in nurses. It looked very nice between her slender hands, and even Comrade Doctor had raised no objection to it.

That was the saddest thing I ever saw, the boy thought. So sad that I shall never chase it out of my head. It is, therefore, fine to have the photograph, though it was taken many years ago. Mama was young then, and she used to smile very often. Later on she began to look older, and, when she smiled, wrinkles ran down the sides of her mouth. Only her eyes stayed young and had the colour of the cloudy sky.

No one should be alone when he is young, the boy thought. But I was alone very often. Mama used to spend in a factory the time of daylight and she washed the clothing of other people until late in the night. Sometimes the boy was allowed to stay up a little longer, and he had truly enjoyed those nights. While Mama was singing he let his hands drop into the blueness of the rinsing water. This had probably been the first time the boy began to dream of the sea. The colour of the deep sea must look like the rinsing water, he reasoned.

Many fortunate peoples have their own seas, he thought with envy. Others have to share a big ocean among themselves. But oceans are of immense size spreading across the wide world. There is a place upon their huge bodies even for me, he assured himself.

That's where I'm going to go to, he said almost aloud. First I shall scrub the deck of a big ship. Perhaps, I'll choose an English vessel. They were the fiercest pirates and had no fear of the savage storms. Then I'll have a boat of my own.

He thought of how the deep blue of the ocean would resemble the dark blue of the rinsing water. The slender clouds floating effortlessly in the light of the dying moon would look like Mama.

Then I should never be sad, he said to himself. I should always be happy. I should even let the exercise book fall into the waves, and fearless sharks would swallow all my sadness that I had written into it.

'But tomorrow you better be confident,' he said aloud. 'For tomorrow all things will be at stake.'

The fat man came to his table with a bowl of soup in his hand, and the boy smacked his lips in anticipation.

'I hope I shan't get you in trouble,' he whispered.

'Your kind always get others in trouble,' the fat man whispered back in an angry, low voice.

'I am sorry.'

'That's all your kind can say: "Sorry, I am sorry."
You should have been sorry before you caused the
trouble. Look at the damage your kind did to
Budapest. I'd bet you were one of them; playing the
role of a hero and stuff like that.'

The soup smelled beautifully, and the boy began
to eat it.

'Of course,' the fat man continued, 'when the fun
is over your kind can't face the music. You quit as
rats do when the ship is sinking.'

The boy thought of the sea and managed a faint
smile.

'I'll go far,' he reassured the fat man.

'Good riddance. Show me your back before you
go so I can give you a farewell kick.'

'I'll do that,' the boy promised cheerfully. 'But
first I need more food. Something solid like
goulash with plenty of dumplings.'

'You'll get nothing more.'

'I'll go very far,' the boy repeated sadly.

'That's what your kind usually do. Go very far
leaving their old parents in shame.'

'I have no parents,' the boy said simply.

The fat man looked at the dirty, grey walls, then
back to the boy.

'Ah,' he said and shrugged his shoulders.

I wonder what he is going to do, the boy thought after the fat man had walked away. This soup is good, though Mama used to cook better ones. But it is hot and it will warm me up. Of course I need the goulash badly, for it would give me strength that I need so much. I'll tear a clean page out of the book and roll a few dumplings in it. If I kept them in my trouser pocket they would not freeze solid. Then I could go on for another three days.

But it is only tomorrow I have to reckon with, he realized. Once in Austria the Americans will give me food packed in neat tins. They say one can take as many as one wishes. I'll take a great deal and go to the English who live on an island and have ships of all sizes.

For a moment he wondered what the big sea will really look like. Is the Red Sea red? And the Yellow Sea as yellow as this soup? If it were so, then the spoon could stand for a frigate and the carrots for angry sharks. The little red beans could represent the friendly turtles.

There is nothing else in the soup, he thought sadly. It's a pity that there is no rice in it. It could be the smaller fish. But I can always imagine that the

16

sharks have eaten them up. That way my soup can be a real sea. And I shall eat them all: the sea, the turtles, the sharks and the little fish in them.

The fat man returned before the boy could finish eating the soup. He brought the plate of goulash and was accompanied by a woman.

'Sit here, Comrade,' the fat man said to the woman. Then he turned to the boy. 'Hurry up and be off.' After some pause he smiled at the woman. 'Don't take any notice of the boy. He is a rag-bag. Call me if he annoys you.'

The woman nodded but did not speak.

She is nice, the boy thought. Almost as nice as Mama. But she looks much younger. Even her eyes look like Mama's, though her hair is lighter in colour. I wonder whether she has the same voice.

That thought made the boy sad. How could he tell? He had forgotten Mama's voice. Why does one remember the face and why does one forget the voice of the dead? I must make her talk. Perhaps her voice is like Mama's. Perhaps if she spoke I would remember.

'Are you not going to eat?' he asked.

'No, I'm not, Comrade. I am only having a cup of coffee.'

17

'Please, don't call me Comrade. Call me boy. Or little boy if you so please.'

'That's very nice of you, little boy. And my name is —'

'Don't. You must not say it,' the boy interrupted hastily. 'One must not say one's real name. It is dangerous. It can get one into trouble.'

'I see ... '

And the young woman smiled. It was a girlish smile; friendly and restrained, yet it displayed permanent sadness.

It is a pity that she must lie, the boy thought. She must be living in fear. I know fear and I always lie when I have fear in my chest. She must be hungry. Her stomach is swollen, and everyone can see that she is with child.

'You must eat.'

'I am not hungry, little boy.'

'You are hungry. Mothers are always hungry.'

'You are very clever,' the young woman said.

'I know a great deal about these things. My Mama was always hungry when she was carrying me under her heart.'

'You said that very beautifully.'

18

'That's not my saying. It was my Mama's. I only remember it fairly well.'

'She must be very proud of you.'

'She is dead.'

'Oh … I am sorry.'

'I am sorry too. But soon I shall not be so sorry. I'll go far and be a sailor. Perhaps I'll work for the English.'

'I hope you will succeed, little boy.'

'I shall,' the boy said with true pride. 'Some day I'll have my own ship and I'll name it after my Mama. Then, I'm sure, my sadness will leave me.'

'And what name will you give to your boat?'

For a moment the boy hesitated, then he said:

'I suppose I can tell you Mama's name. She is dead. No one can hurt her now.'

The woman took out a handkerchief and lifted it to her wet eyes.

'There is much smoke in here,' she remarked in a barely audible voice.

The boy knew that she was crying but said nothing. For some time he kept his eyes glued to the big plate of goulash as if to say farewell to it, then pushed it before the woman.

'If you eat this I'll tell you the name of my Mama.'

'I can't,' the woman sobbed quietly.

'Neither can I,' the boy lied bravely. 'This would be my third meal today.'

The woman looked at the thin, gaunt figure of the boy and said:

'Little boy, we shouldn't lie to each other.'

'We shouldn't.'

'Then why do you say that you have eaten three meals today?'

'Because I have,' the boy said stubbornly.

'You are not telling me the truth.'

'I shall. After you have eaten the goulash.'

'I'll do so if you take a half of it.'

'What for? I ate plenty for lunch.'

What did you eat? the woman thought. Your face is haggard and your hollow eyes speak of great hunger. You have not had a decent meal in weeks. How can I be so thoughtless? How can I let you go on with this gruesome farce of chivalry? I should be ashamed of myself.

She took the big, wooden spoon and filled the soup plate with dumplings and meat.

'Now we are even. I'll eat half of your supper and you'll tell me the name of your mother.'

For a moment the boy sat in silence. Then he began to eat. He ate slowly and chewed every bit well. It's a pity, he thought, that pepper is hard to get. But the fat man had put plenty of paprika into the goulash and it tasted quite good without pepper. When he finished eating he licked the plate clean and pushed it away.

'This is her picture,' he said holding up the tinted photograph.

The woman took it gently.

'She was very beautiful.'

'I know,' the boy said. 'And her name was Maria.'

'I like that name.'

'I liked it too,' the boy said quietly. 'I liked it very much. Though many women have the same name.'

'That's true. Perhaps, because it was the name of Christ's Mother,' explained the woman as she handed the photograph back to the boy.

'Perhaps,' the boy replied drily.

They paused.

'Have you ever heard of Christ?' the woman broke the silence.

'Sometimes. My Mama used to pray to Him.'

'And you? Have you ever prayed to Him?'

'Sometimes,' the boy replied carefully. 'Some time ago. But not since Mama died.'

'Why is that?'

'He never hears me. He must be far away. Perhaps,
when I'm on the sea I shall pray to Him.'

Neither of them felt able to speak any longer. The
boy was thinking of the sea, and he saw himself
standing before the mast on a small ship. Great

22

waves were rolling by and fell down roaring into the wells that they dug for themselves. The sea can kill you, the boy thought, but she can never imprison you. You will be free even though you may be at the mercy of the winds. Yes, the sea is my true friend even though she may kill me.

The fat man returned without the coffee.

'Comrades,' he said, 'I must ask you to leave. A great many people are waiting to be served and I must accommodate them.'

'I see,' the woman said and took up her only luggage. It was a small coffer which had once seen better days and was made of good leather. The boy spread out his blanket and took out the little exercise book. He hid it under his shirt and threw the blanket around his shoulders.

The icy December winds bit into their cheeks as they walked up the street together. The boy loved to hear the hard snow pop under his oversize shoes and he kept stepping merrily, throwing his feet forward with happy force.

'You have no overcoat,' the woman said sympathetically. 'You must be freezing.'

'I have the blanket,' the boy replied, with his head hung down. 'And if I'm cold I shiver myself warm.'

'You will be a brave sailor, little boy.'

Now, the boy smiled for the first time.

'Why don't you come with me?' he asked the young woman. 'The English have great ships with plenty of places on them. There will be a place for

you and for your baby, too. There is a place for
everyone on the big seas. And when I have my
own ship I'll take you on to an island where there

25

is summer all the time. There is such an island.'

'There is,' the woman said quietly.

As they reached the first intersection the woman stopped.

'Goodbye, little boy, and good luck.'

'Good luck,' the boy said. He lifted his right foot, then put it down again, nervously moving it back and forth, feeling the big cobble-stones under the grotesque, oversize shoe. Then he began to walk off, but came back again, as if there were something more he had to say. The wind took hold of his blanket and tried to tear it off his shoulders. It was blowing so hard that it pushed the boy well back. But the boy was a fighter, and he had summoned all his strength to regain the lost ground. He rolled the blanket about his body as sailors furl a sail close to the mast. Then he held it there firmly, pressing its wrinkled ends on to his stomach. The skin was broken on his blue hand and it had the creased scars of frostbite. The woman saw the boy's hand and started to cry.

'You haven't much faith,' the boy said quietly.

'Little boy—' the woman sobbed bitterly—'I wish I had never met you.'

She likes me, the boy thought triumphantly. I am

quite sure she does. I know it. On the high bed, in
the hospital, when Mama found out she was going to
die she also wept, saying: 'Oh, I wish I had never
had you.'

People who really like me, the boy reasoned with
solemn pride, wish that I had never been born.

'Come with me,' he said to the woman. 'I know a
shack in which cattle were sheltered some days ago.
I lived with them for seven days, but, last Monday,
the soldiers came and took them away. Now I
am alone.'

Actually, the shack was a cabin made of heavy
timber and had a dirt floor thickly covered by dry
straw which looked clean and had not smelled badly.
After the cows were gone, the boy had cleaned the
shack, taking out the cow excrement and turning
over the hay with the help of a long-handled pitchfork which he found in the shack.

'Have you mice in here?' the woman asked, looking
about carefully.

'None,' the boy lied in a clear ringing voice. 'The
cows had lice and so had the soldiers who came for
them. But there are no mice in here.'

'And have you any?'

'What?'

'Lice.'

'I don't think so,' the boy replied thoughtfully. 'If I had any they would have bitten me.'

'I expect you are right,' the woman meditated, then she asked in a gentle voice:

'For how long have you been living here, little boy?'

'Since the last Sunday of November.'

'That makes twelve days, for today is Thursday.'

'I suppose it is,' the boy said, 'though I don't know for sure. I only know Sunday. It is the day when the peasants go to church and the soldiers get drunk.'

'And you?'

'I go to church with the peasants.'

'That's a very nice thing to do, little boy.'

'And it is also very good. I'm always hungry on Sundays. But I take the Blessed Sacrament from the Catholics and then I walk over to the Protestants who give me bread and wine. It is a pity Catholics don't give bread but a thin cake of wafer.'

'You shouldn't do things like that, little boy.'

'I know I shouldn't, but they let me do it. Once I knelt down twice at that little fence that is around the altar.'

'Did the priest not recognize you?'

'Oh, yes, he did. For a moment he stopped and said something in Hungarian. Then he said other things in Latin and gave me the little wafer the second time.'

'What did he say?'

'I can't remember now. It was something nice, for he had not looked angrily.'

'Perhaps he took pity on you.'

'Perhaps.'

'But God Himself, is He going to forgive you?'

'How can I hurt Him?' the boy asked sadly. 'I am but little and He is so great.'

The woman felt tired. In the corner of the shack there was a large pile of straw which looked a somewhat orderly heap resembling the contour of a bed. She knelt down and felt the depth of the stack with her outstretched hands. Drawing some straw towards her, and supporting the weight of her body with her left arm, she sat down. She would have liked to be alone now, for she knew she would have another attack of dizziness and, perhaps, of nausea, with a strong impulse to vomit. A sudden contraction of muscles caused a sharp pain in her back, and she bent forward to relieve it.

'Are you feeling sick?' the boy asked anxiously.

'I'll be all right,' the woman said as she straightened up.

The boy looked at her and felt sad. The smile went out of her eyes, he noticed. Though it was a sorrowful smile the boy liked it, for it reminded him of his Mama.

She needs warmth, he thought. She needs plenty of wholesome sunshine. And she mostly needs the soft, salty breeze of the sea. The sea is far away, but I'll get her there. Now I only wish I could make a fire. I could light some straw, but it would not give much warmth. It would fill the shack with smoke which might make her vomit.

The woman uttered a hollow moan and held out her hands in a gesture of desperate supplication. The boy took them gently and pulled her up. Then he began to walk her towards the door, shifting the weight of her body to his gaunt shoulders.

But he did not follow the woman out in the night. People should be left alone when shame visits them, he thought. He remembered how he was once humiliated by rude passers-by when they caught him urinating outside the Hall of Culture. There was a soldier among the mob who unsheathed his bayonet and threatened to cut off a certain part of his body.

An old woman who spoke strange words to the soldier saved him. The boy did not understand what she was talking about, but all those who stood by did, and they soon left the scene laughing heartily.

That is, perhaps, why I like women better than men, he thought. Men are too strong and always act violently. They despise the weak and look down on the unfortunate. They like to spend their time in smoke-filled taverns where drinks are served to make them drunk. How different the sailors must be, the boy reasoned with pride. They have no time to prey upon the feeble, for they have to face the hazards of the mighty oceans.

The woman came back and sat down quietly.

'Now,' she said when she had regained her sad smile, 'I feel much better. I thank you for helping me out, little boy. I also thank you for having stayed inside.'

'You're welcome,' the boy said simply. He picked up a bottle from the dirt floor and gave it to the woman. There was melted snow in it which was clean and icy-cold.

'Thank you, little boy. Let us save the rest.'

'We have tons of it,' the boy said happily, making a sweeping movement with his right arm. 'You can see it on the fields, in the forest and in the clouds above the forest.'

'Snow?' the woman gasped in surprise.

'It is. But fear not; it is clean, for it has come down from the sky.'

Oh, my confident little Robinson Crusoe, the woman thought, it surely fell out of the sky, but you picked it up from the soiled ground where you and your friends, the cows, trod about.

The boy had no knowledge of what the woman was thinking about, but he feared that the thought of drinking snow might nauseate her and she would vomit again and lose more of her strength.

'Have you ever been in the forest?' he asked changing the subject.

'Not in this one,' the woman said shaking her head. 'But I have been in a wild, dark forest where the trees grew higher than any I had ever seen before. There were wildcats and big grey wolves in that forest, angry boars with long, filthy snouts and cinnamon bears with stout, heavy bodies.'

'Did you live there?'

'No. My father used to take me there when I was about as old as you are now.'

'Is he dead now?' the boy asked politely.

32

'He is. And so is my mother whom we lost shortly after my birth.'

How funny, the boy thought. When she was a little girl she had a good father, but had never known her mother. I had my Mama, but never knew my father. Of course my Mama could never afford to take me to a real forest to see the bears, the boars and the grey wolves. But on one day, she had found paper money in a gutter and became so happy that she took me to the Zoo on the following Sunday. There I saw a great number of animals and ate two ice-creams and drank a sweet, lovely drink which was made of real oranges. From the Zoo I brought home a little book which was filled with beautiful pictures of animals and birds. I kept the book for three years and gave it away only four weeks ago. But I didn't mind giving it away, for I presented it to a quiet little girl who was run down by a tank near the Elizabeth Bridge. The doctors cut her legs off and she would be in the hospital for a long time.

But the book will cheer her up, the boy said to himself, the book will surely cheer her up.

They had no light in the shack, and as the moon set below the forest the boy could almost hear, in the night, the cold creeping through the walls. He walked to the small window and looked out to check the stars. They were bright and looked more spread out across the sky than ever before.

This is a bad sign, the boy thought. It is the sign of bad weather: very cold tomorrow; high winds and snow-storm the day after. Perhaps the blizzard will not wait for a full day and will strike tomorrow.

Of course if one is on the run there is nothing sinister about a blizzard. No one can see far enough in a snow-storm, not even the soldiers. It blinds, it covers, it confuses completely. Dogs can hardly pick up one's scent, and if they do so they lose it immediately. The blizzard is my true friend, the boy thought, God knows how much I love it. God knows how much I have been waiting for it.

I know the signs of its coming. Great clouds will rise above the forest like angry mountains. They will be heavy and grey in colour and they will move slowly and very painfully. Then, out of nowhere, the wind will rush forth with insolent fury, showing haughty disregard of the clouds, shaking them off the sky.

Then I and my friend the blizzard shall commence our great struggle. It will bite into my skin and it will chill my bones. I shall shiver and I shall curse it, but step by step I shall gain ground.

But the woman! the little boy thought. What will happen to the woman? I am thin like the slender bow of the great ships that cuts through the rolling waves. But the woman carries a big weight. She is bulky, her steps are clumsy and there is no strength in her legs.

'I must make the woman stronger,' he spoke aloud.

In the corner, upon the high pile of straw, the woman was sleeping. She was lying on her side, and her face looked thoughtful, almost stern. The boy was standing by her, watching her closely. How does the baby lie in the darkness of her body? he pondered carefully. It too must be lying on its side and it must be a girl. The woman has me already. What would she want another boy for?

Yes, I'm sure that it is a girl. Perhaps she is moving right now, and I could feel her if I placed the palm of my hand upon the woman's stomach. But the woman would then wake and that would serve no purpose. She must have rest because rest will strengthen her body. Tomorrow my friend the blizzard will embrace her, and God help her if she is not strong enough.

35

I wish the cows were here, he daydreamed. The shack would be much warmer and I could serve the woman warm milk for breakfast. The baby girl that feels so secure in the warmth of her body would so much enjoy the sweet cow milk. It would pour down to her with all its goodness and it would make her love me for it. Perhaps she knows that I am her brother and that I shall take her on to an island where there is summer all the time.

But what will my friend the blizzard do to her tomorrow? Will it batter her gentle body against the bones of her mother, or will it chill her into a sad little corpse?

He picked up an armful of straw and covered the woman with it.

'Sleep, little sister,' he said to the unborn babe. 'Let us hope that my friend the blizzard will show its mercy tomorrow. Let us hope that his father, who is the Great Wind of the Seven Seas, will not push his son too strongly. Make yourself into a warm bundle now, and sleep, little sister.'

Then he went back to the tiny window and looked out again. Outside there was a clear night. Pale starlight swept the snow clean as far as his eyes could see. Not far, perhaps a kilometre away, the forest, filled with cold and uneasy darkness, stretched itself.

The boy remembered the fairy tales his mother used to tell, and he shuddered. This forest was not the forest of which Mama spoke in her quiet voice. This forest was a giant that lay menacingly in his path; between him and the English who had great ships of all sizes. This forest was not inhabited by shrewd witches with whom one could strike a bargain. It housed no dwarfs one could befriend. This forest was empty. It was covered half in snow, half in frozen leaves. Its trees held out their white branches, luring on and pushing away the trespassers. And it had high teeth that were made of tall timber and that housed the soldiers with their short bar-relled guns which made an ugly noise and which dealt quick death.

But my friend the blizzard will blind them, the boy thought hopefully. It will fill their eyes with crystals that are sharp as the point of a needle. It will force them down in search for shelter. It will tear their long, hairy coats and freeze their ears to their helmets. It will help me to meet its father who roams the seven seas and who will fill the sails of my ship.

But will the woman like the blizzard? How can I

explain it to her? How can I tell her that it is my friend and her friend also? How can I tell my little sister, whose ears are deafened by the woman's bulky body, that my friend the blizzard is her friend too, even though it may chill her tiny wet body to numbness?

'I can't talk to my little sister,' the boy spoke out aloud, 'but I can make the woman who carries her strong.'

He judged the time by the stars and realized that it was midnight.

If I had more brains, he thought, I would have got more food from the fat man. But then I would have lost the woman who was in a great hurry. I needed the woman's friendship more than food. Still it was foolishness. The fat man would have given me more food had I pestered him hard enough. He was a man of loud voice and of angry outbursts. Yet it is not his type I am afraid of. I fear those who never raise their voice. He who shouts now may laugh in the next moment. But he who speaks in an even voice has no mercy in his heart. I do not understand these things, he thought, but it was a good thing that the fat man did not have a smooth face and eyes that hardly blinked.

38

It is too late now. The fat man is sleeping behind locked doors. Everybody is sleeping behind closed doors: the woman, my little sister and even the forest. But I and my bright lanterns, the stars, are awake. I am taking care of the woman, but who is taking care of me? And who is taking care of the stars? If there is no one to look after them, then the stars are my brothers, for they are alone in spite of all their greatness and their glory.

He thought of how long the stars would live. In September he watched many die. They burst out of the sky, and as they fell they burnt their lives away in ember-yellow rays. When a star dies, the boy thought sadly, the whole world watches it in awe. But when my Mama died it was only I who felt sadness. It is true that some of the nuns wept with me and made me say three Hail Marys. But I was so sad that I could not remember the prayer. Luckily the nuns said them so fast that they did not notice that I mixed the Hail Marys with the Lord's Prayer.

But I was sure Mama did not mind my careless Hail Marys. Just as I am sure that she does not feel angry now about my friendship with the woman. It was a pity that I could not look after Mama the way

I am looking after the woman. But I was much younger when Mama lived.

Now I am older and clear-headed enough. And I know that in life food is needed as much as love.

I must get food for the woman. There is nothing accomplished with daydreaming, the boy thought.

Perhaps the creek, now that it has been frozen since last Monday, will give up some fish. It is a small, straight stream almost without a turn or winding and it is not far off. Fish like calm waters, and the creek has a steady, smooth surface which has never been distorted by the swirls of a current. Its floor is padded with soft mud which is the favourite hiding-place of the large-scaled carp.

Carps grow to a big size, the boy remembered, to

41

give himself confidence, and they live to a great age. It is true that I worked the creek for a full week and caught nothing, but I had no bait except for a few half-frozen berries. They were red and sweet-smelling, but the carp could not smell them and it left them untouched. But, he thought, the creek is frozen now, and if I cut a hole in its hard armour the carp will come up to catch a mouthful of fresh air.

He took a length of string that hung on a nail on the wall. It was about nine feet long and had a piece of wire, which was curved like a hook, tied to its end.

'That will do,' he said. 'You'll have lovely and cold berries at the point, carp. You won't be so fussy tonight. Since you have the ice above your head, carp, you take anything that is given to you.'

Of course, the boy thought, it would be a different matter if I had a net or even an old pan. The carp will jump to take air, and a net could catch it in mid-air with ease. But I have neither a net nor a pan. I have nothing.

He wound the piece of string into a neat coil, then took the long-handled pitchfork which he needed for an ice-breaker.

I should take the blanket, he thought. It must be very cold outside and it will be half past one before I come back. That is, of course, if the carp comes up early. But it must come up. It will see the light of the stars and, if it is stupid enough, it will think that spring is here. When it jumps I can hit it with the pitchfork. Just as I would hit a ball with a bat.

But then he decided not to take the blanket. It would hinder me, and perhaps it would get wet, he thought. I could tuck it into my trousers, but then it would keep falling off my shoulder. I need precision and concentration. The carp will jump but once. I can't afford to miss it. Therefore I shall leave the blanket in the cabin and cover the woman with it.

When he had done so, he left the cabin.

Outside he could smell the strong smell of pine trees that a light breeze brought from the west. He loved the smell of pine trees, for it made him remember Christmas. His Mama used to buy a small tree every Christmas, and while the boy was sleeping she smuggled it into the little room. But the boy had only pretended that he was asleep, for he did not want to embarrass his Mama. They lived in a single room in which there were a bed, two chairs, an oven and a table. Upon this table, into an old bucket, Mama placed the small tree. Then she cut the large sheets of a newspaper into lovely patterns and covered the rusty body of the bucket with them. After this had been done, she usually stepped back and looked at the naked tree from a distance. She needed time to decide where to put the few broken glass ornaments which she carefully guarded in an old shoe-box during the year. After the shiny balls had been placed in their proper position she sat down by the half-dressed tree and commenced to cut long strips of paper out of the coloured covers of old foreign magazines.

Soon the tree was ready, as compact and bullet-shaped as a rocket waiting to soar to Heaven. Finally, Mama hung her rosary upon the highest twig and knelt down to say her sad prayers.

The boy had never understood that. Why did Mama pray when prayer made her look unhappy? Why did Mama say her prayers when no one would ever hear them?

He did not truly feel good seeing Mama praying. Priests pray a great deal, he thought, but people pray only when they have no hope in their heart. Happy people laugh, sing and swear, for they have friends, hopes, and their bellies are warm and full.

But Mama was sad and tired and there was nothing else she could do against sorrow. So she prayed.

On Christmas morning, the boy remembered, he woke up quite early, but wanted his mother to witness his joy, so he went back to sleep again. Though he knew that there would be no presents under the tree he did not feel badly about it, because he had Mama's company for the whole day. Then for lunch they ate roast veal with baked potatoes. In the afternoon they drank hot milk into which they dropped small pieces of soft white cake. When the evening came, Mama lighted the candles on the tree and sang carols. She had a lovely voice, and the boy liked to listen to it. Soon the small candles burnt their lives away, and Mama blew them out one by one. Finally darkness reigned in the little room, yet, holding hands, they could see the tree clearly with the light that came in from the yellow street lamps.

It makes me so lonely to think about these things, the boy thought sadly, but I cannot help it. The breeze that brings the smell of young pine trees into my nostrils is at fault.

He was walking steadily. It was no effort for him because the snow was soft and only ankle-deep. The stars seemed to hang much higher now, and they hardly ever blinked. Perhaps it will be colder still, the little boy said, watching the

45

stars, as he trod along the path that led to the bushes.

'I trust there will be some berries left,' he said aloud. The birds might have eaten some of them, but I hope that they have left a few for me. A dozen is all I need, perhaps less. My greatest hope is that the carp will jump. If he stays down I must use the hook. But the carp may not take the hook and then I shall never catch it.

But I must catch it, and I must kill it. The woman needs another meal before my friend the blizzard arrives.

The bush had plenty of berries, and the boy filled his pockets with them. This is my lucky night, he thought happily, and with good luck I cannot fail to hook the carp.

Just then he heard a faint noise which gave him a fright and made him jump back. It came from under the bush, and the boy held out his right arm in a blind gesture of self-defence. Then with both hands he grabbed the pitchfork and stepped forward bravely.

It can't be bigger than a fox, he whispered hope-fully.

It was smaller than that. It was a rabbit.

'Hullo there,' the boy said.

The rabbit did not move but twitched his nose in a friendly manner.

'Where are you from? Are you living around here? If not, what brought you here? Hunger? If so, you are my little brother.'

He is not afraid of me, the boy realized. He is very brave. Or perhaps he is half frozen and sees a friend in an enemy. But I am not an enemy of his, and I would not hurt him for anything in this world.

'Fear me not, little brother,' he said gently. 'Fear not and trust me. No harm will come to you. Don't even think of that. You are lonely and hungry and that makes you my little brother. Here, have some berries. The birds left plenty for us.'

All my life I wanted a pet, the boy thought while he watched the rabbit chewing the berries. But Mama and I lived in a small room in which there was no place for a pet. Once I brought home a puppy dog which I had found abandoned outside the school building. I kept it for three days in the community washroom, but the rude-faced man who was the commissar of the building in which we lived, told me to get rid of it. I found a new home for the puppy, giving it to a schoolmate of mine whose father was a policeman. They lived in the suburbs and they could

47

call a lovely back garden their own. At that time I envied my schoolmate for having a fine father who could provide him with a spacious garden. But the angry people who roamed the streets last October hanged his father upon an old oak tree. It was an ugly sight, for the noisy men had not only hanged him, but kicked his dead body too, until it became blue and pinkish. Then they spat on it.

I felt a true sorrow for my friend and wanted to say nice things to him, but I just could not remember the soft words the kind nuns said to me at my Mama's funeral. So I told him about my own sadness.

But my own sorrow had not relieved him from his great distress.

'Your Mama was killed by God,' he said to me sadly, 'and you can't hate God. You just don't see Him. But they were men who killed my father, and I can see them walking the streets leading their own children by the hand. Oh, why, why did they do that to me?'

Why? the boy thought while he fed the rabbit with crimson berries. Why does everything have to kill everything else in some way or another? God killed my Mama; I shall have to kill the carp, and

48

my friend the blizzard will do his utmost to kill us all tomorrow: the woman, my little sister, me and the rabbit.

Yes, the rabbit too. Because I shall take him with me. I shall live on a big ship sailing on the broad back of the mightiest ocean. There will be plenty of room for the rabbit.

But now I must catch him and take him back to the cabin.

He knelt down and held the berries lightly in his left hand. Then he began to work his way on his knees towards the rabbit, being cautious not to frighten him away. The rabbit beheld him with friendly contempt and became alarmed only when the boy grabbed him by the skin of his neck.

'Now, don't be afraid, little rabbit,' the boy said starting to walk back towards the cabin. 'I'm your brother and will protect you. Tonight you'll sleep in the dry, warm cabin, and next morning you'll get more berries. You may eat of the carp too if you think that it would do you good.'

The rabbit stopped struggling and settled himself peacefully on the boy's chest. Only his ears twitched nervously as if they had listened to the boy's caressing words.

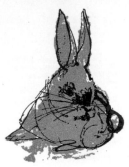

'Rabbit, one day you will be happy that we have met. For I shall take you to a sunny island where you can chew thick, ever-green grass and sweet-smelling grubs all the time. There is such an island, rabbit.'

He offered another berry to the rabbit, but he
refused to take it.

'Ah, well, your feelings are hurt. I understand,' the
boy said in his gentlest voice. 'But you're not a
prisoner of mine. You'll be one of our family. You'll

51

meet the woman, and my little sister who lives in the woman's body.'

The rabbit made a weak attempt to escape, but the boy held him firmly in his arms.

I shall not talk to him any more, the boy thought, because my voice is upsetting him. Probably he has every right to fear man, although he showed no signs of fear when we met. Perhaps he can think just as I can, and in that case he must suffer a lot. He needs a good sleep now, and I hope that he will dream of the bullet that might have killed him one day.

Tomorrow, my friend the blizzard will howl some sense into his slender ears. It will teach him that love is protection and aloneness invites early death.

The squeaking of the door woke the woman.

'Who is that?' she asked sleepily.

'I and a friend,' the boy answered.

'A friend?' The woman sat up alarmed.

'An animal friend, not a human one.'

'Thank God for that,' the woman said, relieved, and sank back into the imprint made by her body upon the high pile of straw.

The boy brought the rabbit nearer to her.

'She is sweet.'

'It is a he, not a she.'

52

'Pardon me: I cannot see him on account of the darkness.'

'I did not truly examine him either. I only feel that he is a male.'

The woman smiled.

'Perhaps you err,' she said softly.

'I cannot. I feel strongly that he is a boy just as I am one.'

'You are a strange little boy.'

And you are a strange woman, too, the boy thought. You have not yet said anything about yourself. It is true that you wanted to tell your name, but I did not really care to hear it. Names are of no import and they can be easily made up.

But you carry my little sister within your tired body and I wonder where her father is? If he is dead I have no reason to fear him. If he is alive, waiting for you at the other side of the forest, he may not want me. Of course, I am not afraid of aloneness. I lived alone for quite a long time, and now I have the rabbit who will be a good friend to me.

'Why don't you lie down and sleep, little boy?' the woman asked in a drowsy voice which was heavy with sleep.

'I have to finish my business.'

'And what is your business?'

To make you strong, the boy thought. To lead you through the fury of my friend the blizzard. To reunite you with him who may wait for you at the other end of the silent forest.

Now the boy paused, then he spoke out:

'Are you alone?'

'I am with you,' the woman said quietly.

'You are now. But will you be alone the day after tomorrow?'

'I shall be if you leave me.'

The boy put the rabbit down. It crawled instinctively to the woman's warm body. She dragged it under the blanket.

'Why do you ask, little boy?'

'I thought you had a man who would be waiting for you.'

'If I had a man he would be near me. But I have only you, little boy.'

I am glad, the boy thought. Shifting the weight of his body from one of his legs to the other he paused hesitatingly. Should he ask the question that puzzled him so much?

'Is he dead?' he asked finally.

'Is who dead?'

'Your husband.'

The woman placed her left hand under the chin of the rabbit. For a moment she stared at its agile little nose. Then she said bravely:

'I am not married.'

Silence fell between them. They could clearly hear the sound that the rabbit was making trying to dig itself into the straw.

It's a good thing we have the rabbit, the boy thought. We can fix our gaze upon its funny little head and do not have to look into each other's eyes. Of course, the shame is on me, for it is I who have asked that question. The woman is honest, therefore she answered it. I do not know much about these things; all I know is that people look down upon women whose children are born without a man to give them a name. That this is unjust and stupid even I can see. But people do not see it that way, and the woman might think that I was just one of those people.

I must think of something.

He lifted his eyes off the rabbit and looked up. His glance met the woman's searching stare. Without thinking he said in a low voice:

'My Mama wasn't married either.'

Now, what made me say this shameful lie? he thought, as he felt his heart throbbing in his throat. His body began to shiver under the shock-waves of his blood that beat strongly and fast, and he felt sobs break through his gasping breath.

'I must finish my business,' he blurted out curtly.

Outside the cabin he started to run towards the creek, dragging the long-handled pitchfork in the soft snow as if it were a device made for slowing the great motion of his excitement.

The breeze was fresher now and it threw the brisk odour of the pine trees in his face. It made the boy think of Christmas again, and he felt tears run down his cheeks.

'I wronged Mama and I wronged the woman,' he sobbed bitterly.

He rubbed the tears away with an awkward movement of his left hand. The thin film of fluid spread across his face and soon commenced to freeze because of the cold air.

'I don't mind it, I don't mind anything from now on,' he wept out aloud. 'I wronged Mama just because I wronged the woman.'

Why must everything wrong everything else in

this world? A man, unknown to me, wronged the
woman and I made up for it by wronging Mama.
Strong men often wronged me, so I wronged the fat
man because he had a weak will.

The icy cold breeze found his open mouth and
rushed down his throat, causing sharp pains inside
his chest.

Now the wind wrongs me, the boy thought sadly,
but I do not mind. Something might have hurt the
wind, perhaps mighty mountains, far away, and now

it takes revenge on me. But I let its anger tear into my lungs, not because I cannot stop it, but because I deserve just punishment. No one can chastise me but the wind. Mama is dead, the woman is gentle, my little sister is not yet born and the rabbit cannot talk. I have no one else besides them.

'Come on, wind,' he started to yell loudly. 'Come on and stop me if you can. You are but a puny babe. My great friend, the blizzard, and his father who roams the seven seas, are my real sparring partners. You are but a weakling of inferior size and strength.'

That he had humbly begged for chastisement a moment ago meant nothing. Now he was proving again the undaunted spirit of youth. Now he was proving that he was a born fighter. Now he was ready to find the carp and to kill it mercilessly.

The creek was only a couple of hundred yards away, and the boy decided that it was bad for him to run the remaining distance. He feared that his running and thumping would scare the carp away. I must be cautious, using great cunning. The carp itself is cunning. If it is fully grown it must be very old. Old creatures know fear better than young ones, and they also know the tricks that preserve life in the constant shadow of mortal danger.

58

But I am a man, and man knows mightier tricks. Clever though it is, the carp will fall for them. Of course, I have nothing against the carp. I have not even seen it. If it were living on earth instead of in the water, it could easily become my friend, just as the rabbit became my friend. But it lives in the water, dreaming of the spring and of fat water-bugs. It will take the berries and the hook inside them. If its mouth is large enough it may swallow the hook which will pierce its old heart.

Now the boy reached the creek.

He knelt down and, in a careful manner, made his way towards the ice on his hands and knees. Noise must be avoided at all costs, he thought. Lucky for me that there is a soft blanket of snow on the top of the ice. It acts as a carpet, muffling the thumping of my limbs.

Suddenly he felt the ice hard and slippery under his hands, and he stopped crawling. With his right hand he drew the pitchfork alongside his body. If the ice breaks, he reasoned intelligently, I'll have the pitchfork lying across the crack and I shall be able to pull myself out of the water.

He was happy, feeling the compact hardness of the ice.

59

'You have quite a blanket above your head, carp,' he said. 'I bet you feel high winter coming with its grinding frost. But I will confuse you, carp, by cutting a window in the ceiling of your prison. I'll cut it large so that the stars will be able to look down at you in comfort. I'll cut it large so that you'll be compelled to rise out of the icy water. Then, with your body filled with small sacs of air, you won't go down too far. Curiosity will make you rise again and you shall never re-enter your prison. The first time I may miss you, but that will mean nothing, for I shall surely get you the second time.'

But first, the boy thought, I must cut a hole in the ice. It would be foolish to stand up without knowing for sure how thick the ice is. So I just have to work crawling on my hands and knees.

He cleared the surface of the ice by sweeping the snow away with his bare hands. Then he took his pocket-knife and drew a neat square with it. The knife made a slow, scratching noise, and the boy pressed it against the ice until his arm became stiff and he had to rest it.

What will I do if the carp hears the noise and decides to stay down? What will I do if the blade slits through the ice and the carp catches a glimpse of

60

it? I do not know. Again he commenced to cut the ice, slowly increasing the pressure on the knife, holding it with both of his hands. This time the ice gave up a low, uneasy moan, and the boy knew that he had managed to cut through the thickest part of it.

He put his knife down. Then he took up the pitchfork, lifting it as silently as he could. Holding its handle in both hands he straightened up, allowing his knees to hold the weight of his body.

Then he placed the sharp points of the fork upon the ice as gently as possible and began to push it down again and again with the ever-increasing weight of his arms. Finally the sheet of ice gave way and, with a loud cracking sound, it disappeared under the bulging surface of the creek.

Its sudden momentum caused the water to pour from the sides of the hole, and the boy had no time to escape its unexpected surge. He felt the icy liquid penetrate the coarse material of his trousers.

This is bad, he thought, but dared not stand up. The ice is only one inch thick, he observed, and it may not take the full weight of my body. Of course, I should have been more careful, but it is too late to lament about that. My trouser legs are soaking wet and soon they will freeze solid because of the cold air. I must shift them constantly, so that they will not freeze to the ice-cap of the creek. If Mama were with me, she would now take me home and make me stand in a large bucket that she would have filled with steamy, warm water. Then she would drop a handful of salt and a spoonful of mustard into the water. Then she would rub my back with the big brush she kept under the stove. Then she would tuck me in bed.

But, the boy thought sadly, my Mama is dead and I have no home. I have not even a bucket.

Perhaps the creek meant to play a joke on me. Perhaps it did not know that I would be a sailor and I should sail waters immensely greater in size than the creek itself. Perhaps it knew and it became jealous.

Yet I do not care. I am mightier than the creek. I proved it already by carving an ugly scar upon its smooth face. Now I will kidnap and kill its proud king, the carp, which dwells on its muddy bottom.

Yes, I will kill its king, majestic though it is. I will feed it to the woman whose blood will carry the strong juice of its grey meat into the body of my little sister.

'I am sorry, carp,' he whispered between his teeth. 'I am sorry for you and for your relatives. But you have eaten a great number of small fish in your time. Their death made you grow big, just as your death will make the woman strong. I know this is cruel, carp. I know it as well as you do. But what can you or I do about it? Nothing, carp, nothing. We just go on killing. You killed the smaller fish, I'll kill you; my friend the blizzard will want to kill me tomorrow. Even the stars get killed, carp. Perhaps you, too, have watched them fall and seen their shame written on the sky in crimson letters. And who can read those letters? Nobody, carp, nobody.'

His trouser legs were soon covered with minute crystals of ice and their cold bit into the fleshy back part of his leg between the knee and the ankle.

A cramp is the last thing I want now, the boy thought, shifting his legs from one place to another. Then he got off his knees and sat down. Placing his palms behind his back on the ice, he lifted his legs up, pivoting the weight of his body on the rounded parts of his buttocks. Then he began cycling in the air. The more he kicked the more unpleasant he felt.

'You are traitors, legs,' he mumbled painfully. 'How can you let me down just now? The hole is

63

cut, the carp is beginning to receive the message from the stars, and you make me sit here kicking the air like a clown. What will I do if the carp decides to jump just now? What sort of legs are you two? Will you desert me tomorrow, too, when your strength will be needed to push me head-on into the white fury of my friend the blizzard?'

But his legs disobeyed the boy. They felt numb and deadened with cold. Sharp pains, which seemed to have originated in his calves, shot through his whole body and found their ultimate target in his lungs. He coughed suddenly and noisily.

'Enough of that,' he whispered angrily. 'Enough of that, legs and lungs. You frighten the carp away.'

He lowered his legs and knelt up again. This time, however, he chose a spot farther away from the hole. He picked up the pitchfork, holding it by its long handle. His hands started to shake slightly.

'Oh, hands, don't do that,' he murmured in his dark mood. 'I need precision. I must hit the carp when it jumps.'

But half an hour later he knelt there still, tense and freezing, holding the pitchfork in his hands. The breeze became quite strong now and the boy was happy knowing that his friend the blizzard was

64

moving forth behind it. My friend has a great push, the boy thought, I wish the carp felt it and jumped in its terror.

But the carp did not jump.

'Please, friend,' the boy addressed the carp softly, 'do rise and jump. I promise to kill you quickly and painlessly. I'll hit you on the head and drive the pitchfork through your body. I also promise to bury your bones with reverence. I'll drop them back into the creek and make sure that they sink to the bottom where your relatives can find them and lay them in the soft mud which was your hunting ground for years. It will be a funeral fit for a king — you really are one. But now, please, friend, do not let me wait any longer.'

The handle of the seven bright stars that make up the Plough turned farther away from the Pole Star, and the boy knew it was past two in the morning.

His hands became numb with cold and he found it difficult to move his fingers. He rubbed them with snow which brought life back into them.

But I cannot do anything with my legs, he realized sadly. They are too big and too clumsy. Nothing will help them but the carp. The sooner it

c   65 jumps the better it will be for me and for the legs. If the carp waits, the legs must wait also.

I wonder what the carp does now. And I wonder what it looks like. It must be old and fat. It must have lost many of its large, shiny scales, though it must still look solemn and majestic in its semi-nakedness. How strange that I, a mere boy, had to come here to kill it. Perhaps it preferred to be killed by a strong soldier, or by a king like itself, or by a mighty commissar.

Perhaps.

Somehow I must let it know that I am worthy of its death and I am fit to be its executioner. If it knew that I should soon be killing its fearless and noble cousins, the killer sharks of the great seas, it would rise and jump.

But the carp does not know this.

Perhaps I should show it my face, the boy thought. But it might see that I was young and desperate and it would go back to sleep. I must wait and pray. Maybe my patron saint, Saint Anthony, will help me to kill the carp. He loves the poor.

'Saint Anthony,' he said whispering, 'make the carp jump. I have not much time. My legs are frozen and there is a strange pain under my

66

shoulders. I must kill the carp. I must go back to the cabin. There I must cook the carp and give it to the woman. You help the woman, Saint Anthony, and my little sister who lives in the woman's body.'

But another half-hour went by, and the carp had still not shown itself.

The boy had to crawl away from the hole. He stood up on the solid ground and urinated. When he turned back and went down on his knees and hands in order to crawl back, the carp jumped.

Its body, heavy and rocket-shaped, shot out of the water like a bullet. For a moment it shone brightly in the starlight, and the water which poured from its sides looked like a loose, silvery mantle. It put its full length in view before re-entering its domains.

'You are bigger than I thought,' the boy gasped in awe. 'And you are truly a king wearing your regal robe with dignity.'

But why, oh why, did it have to come up now, he thought. A full hour I spent watching the hole, yet it jumped at the exact time when my cold feet made me urinate. Now it knows that I am but a boy, cold and miserable, a slave of his bladder.

He worked his way back to the hole and picked up the pitchfork again.

'Come on, king,' he said in true anger, 'come on, and jump again. But next time don't be so cocksure, for I shan't miss you.'

If only I could turn time back for two short minutes, he thought desperately. He looked around because he would have liked to find solace in his grief. To his left there stood the forest, silent and impassive; above his head there glowed the stars, remote and serene.

Aloneness is my greatest handicap, the boy thought unhappily, and also the fact that I have no luck. Sometimes someone needs luck more than food. But I have had no luck since Mama died.

Soon the pitchfork became heavier to hold, and the boy kept his hands wide apart on its long handle in order to reduce its ever-increasing weight.

'Either you weigh more, or I'm getting weaker.' He sighed. 'But I must not give up. The carp saw what a young boy I am and now it feels confident. It will want to amuse itself. Let us hope so,' he said.

Yet it is I who am truly confident, he thought, to give himself endurance. The legs do not ache so intensely any more. They have been deprived of the power of feeling. I do not care much about them as long as they are not deadened completely. I let them

68

sleep and I let them have their rest, for I shall need them tomorrow.

And I have more bad news for you, carp. I do not feel the coldness of the night any more. My lungs burn with strong heat as if they were filled with red hot coke. I am warm and confident, carp, more confident than you have ever been. It won't matter now how long I shall have to wait. I'll just wait. And at the end I will surely kill you.

In the meantime, the boy thought, I must think of something else. Perhaps I shall think of the island where there is summer all the time. I shall think of its long golden beach that stretches for one or two miles, and of the sand that covers it and is so hot that it burns one's feet. I shall think of myself coming down on to it in the evening breeze, holding my little sister and leading the rabbit on a piece of string. The moon will be up by then and we shall see the great beauty of the sea and watch its soft body moving up and down as it makes love with the moonlight. Then we shall perceive the flight of the night birds and see them circle and drop and see them churn the water. And when they are gone, we shall still hear their sad little voices crying out in the blueness of the evening.

Yes, we shall do these things, perhaps more, if we can walk through the forest under the white angry blanket of my friend the blizzard.

But we will walk through. The legs will feel fine by tomorrow and I hope that my chest will be as hot then as it is now.

It was getting into the third hour of the morning, and the boy, kneeling and shivering, looked like the portrait of a man broken by neglect and disappointment. Thin and worn, with his Adam's apple protruding from his skinny neck, he looked down at the hole with the humble puzzlement of a dog unjustly beaten.

I wish the carp could know what I really am, and I also wish that it knew the woman, he thought. Now that it has seen me once, it has carried down with it the picture of my poverty and helplessness. I wish it would come up again to take a second look at me. But I'm only wishing, for I cannot do anything else.

Then he thought of the hook and of the berries which he had in his pocket. He dropped down the pitchfork and started to rub his hands with snow. His little fingers became totally numb and he could not move them, but his thumbs and the rest of his

70

fingers responded readily to his will. He took out the neat coil and commenced to dress the hook. Soon the whole of the hook, the point and the shank too, was covered with fresh, solid berries.

Now he began to sink his makeshift fishing line, holding the string between his thumb and finger. Everything now depends on what the carp may think of the bait, he reasoned — and also on what I can endure.

But I can endure a lot. I was born to suffer, and God knows I can take more pain than anybody else. It is better to fight back than to lose one's spirit, he told himself. It is better to go down with anger in one's heart than to accept violence peacefully.

He remembered the misty November morning when the soldiers were hanging people upon the slender spans of the great bridge that stretched over the Danube. The victims were a meek crowd of men, sullen and slow-moving, and not one of them showed resentment. Death must be a force, the boy thought. It must be an enravishment. The impact of it must make man feel lesser than he really is. That is why the poor wretches seemed to walk on air, and that is why the whole world seemed to have stopped in a respectful silence.

71

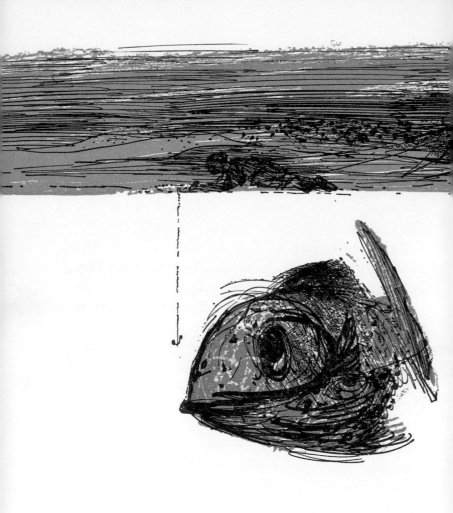

But not I, the boy remembered proudly. I was not
inclined to submission. I sat on the top of an old

chestnut tree and bravely whistled, forcing my breath against my cracked lips. And next morning, when I was taking a walk among the swinging bodies, I talked softly to them, telling them how much I disapproved of their strange behaviour. If only they knew how shameful they would look in death, with their swollen tongues poked out, and with their blue faces expanded as a result of a desperate pressure from within, they would have chosen to die in anger, fighting the soldiers with their bare teeth. Anyhow, they finished up in the river into which their killers threw them on the third day.

Perhaps the carp, too, knows about these things and respects man no more. It may think that men were made to be food for the fish and not the other way round.

'But you just wait, carp. You just wait and see,' the boy said aloud. 'Not all men are at the end of the rope. Not as yet, anyhow. If you don't believe me, so much the worse for you. For you shall yet feel the strength of my arms. But now, you just smell the berries. They are fresh, firm and appetizing. They are yours. All is yours: their sweetness, their goodness and their death which is hidden within them.'

Still kneeling he looked up at the stars carefully. It isn't much more than three o'clock, he decided. Then he leaned over the hole and examined the thickness of the ice. Perhaps, if I stood, keeping my legs wide apart, the ice would not break. But can I trust the ice and can I trust my legs? I cannot. The ice is treacherous and so are my legs.

He would have liked to have something to cushion the hard pressure of the ice. The handle of the pitchfork will not do, he thought. It would break the skin on my buttocks and would bruise my flesh. Of course, if I had more brains I would have built a cosy seat of snow. But it is now too late for that because the hole in the ice cannot be left unguarded. My eyes, my hands and my mind must be alert. It would be difficult to work with the pitchfork while holding the

74

line in one of my hands. But I can deal a mighty blow with my other hand, slapping the carp in the face.

I wish I had magic in my eyes and could see the woman, he daydreamed. She must be sleeping, lying sideways, trying to escape the uneasy weight of my little sister. Do mothers dream of their unborn children? he asked himself. Do they love them in their dreams, too? I cannot tell. But I think they don't. In my dreams I have often killed people whom I have never seen. I think the woman hates my little sister when she dreams of her. She must, because she fears the time of delivery. But when she awakes she sees the beauty of the world around her and feels proud to bring my little sister into it.

Yet, I am quite sure, when her body sleeps and her soul is wide awake, she truly hates that awful weight which is my little sister.

This thought made the boy sad.

'Life is strange,' he said softly as if he were attempting to lure the carp by the mild music in his voice. 'I know because I had many questions no one could answer for me. My Mama just smiled when I asked those questions, and the nuns just prayed. I should have died with Mama in her hour of delivery.

75

Then I should have never known her and aloneness. But life must be like death: an unwanted force. The men who were about to hang on the bridge knew that. So they just placed their necks in the noose. And while I brazenly whistled, sitting on the top of the chestnut tree, they died watching their fellow-condemned kick against the cruel weight of their bodies.

The boy shuddered in extreme disgust. Death may be a relief, he thought, but for those who witness it, it is a shame, a regrettable disgrace. And who is the cause of death? He Who is the cause of life. And, very often, men who just cannot afford to, wait for Him.

And the carp knows these things, too, and regards all men with contempt, including me, who is just a half a man. But I am the one who whistled on the chestnut tree and I shall be the one who will drag its fat body along the snow and frozen clods.

'Sorry, carp,' he said aloud, 'I am sorry to break my promise. But I shall not give you a decent funeral. I will break your old bones under my big shoes which make people laugh. I'll tread on your proud head and leave it half buried in the dirt where the rats can find it.'

But first I must catch you, he realized. He began to pull up the string to examine the hook. The smallest berry, which he put on the point of the hook, was missing. Did the carp eat it, he pondered, or did it disintegrate in the water. It could not have, because the rest of the berries did not lose their wholeness and were firmly impaled by the shank. Either the carp devoured it, or I have lost the art of precision, he thought. In either case it is a sign of bad things to come. Whether it ate up the berry or not, the carp saw the sharp point of the hook. And the carp is an old hunter, a sage potentate, well versed in the wisdom of survival.

I must try it again, the boy thought sadly, though he did not hope to succeed. He pulled a handful of berries out of his pocket and selected the smallest and the hardest one. Then he covered the point with it and dropped the line back into the creek.

'Everything is now up to you, carp,' he said.

Then he turned his head towards the Plough. When I was smaller, he remembered, I thought you were a great cart, heavy and cumbersome, drawn by four archangels. And I pitied the angels because you looked huge, made for rough work. But today I know that you are but stars, and at any minute you may die. Yet you are luckier than men are. You must not eat and, therefore, you can afford to live proudly. Neither must you crawl on your hands and knees to beg for the life of an old fish.

But I must beg for it even though the sight of my humiliation may fill your bright eyes with disgust. One day, however, you will understand these things. It will be the day when a great hand will push you off the sky, causing you to tumble, then to fall. Thus, star, you will know fear as I now know it. So, turn your eyes away and do not look, because I have to go through with it.

Then the boy looked down at the hole and leaned over it.

'Carp,' he said softly, 'this is the proudest moment of your old life.'

Then he felt compelled to pause in search of the right words. He sensed the great significance of the moment, grave and humiliating, but could not mould his thoughts, that were vague and indefinite in their shapes, into an appropriately expressive form. He knew that in his person man had come to a beast, scarcely longer than a foot, to admit his defeat and his desperation. Millions of years before his time, men had learned to supplicate blessings,

78

seeking by earnest prayers and by brute sacrifices the much-wanted assistance of a higher power, real or imaginary. To bow down in a token of respect to an impersonal person man fears, and never has the chance to conquer, is a sad but sometimes gratifying experience. Yet seldom if ever does man truly frustrate himself before a being he can kill, or before a thing he can destroy. To do so, man must face stark disaster, the frightening nearness of which clouds his reason.

'Carp,' the boy said again, 'I implore your help. You have lived to a great age. What more may life hold for you? Another spring? Or perhaps another summer? What do a few more months matter? Not much. One day the stars will look down at your body, and they will see it cast ashore where swarms of flies and hordes of large stink-bugs will devour it.'

The surface of the water commenced to freeze again, and the boy had to break off the thin slices of ice that attached themselves to the sides of the hole. What is ice for?

Protection, he thought, that enables fish to have their long winter sleep. But what sort of protection does it provide when a boy can cut through it? Not to mention the soldiers, who can throw hand-grenades on it, blasting its shiny coat to smithereens, killing the fish that sleep underneath. But he wanted to say nothing of this to the carp for fear of insulting it. The carp needs no ice for a shield. Its great cunning is its protection. My only hope is to pay homage to its cleverness.

'Great king,' he whispered in a low voice filled with reverence. 'I respect you very much. Forgive my trespassing on your time. But I brought you greetings from your majestic cousins, the great sharks of the seven seas, that are built so huge and so strong that they have no fear at all and do what they wish. Yet they look upon you with envy because you have wisdom and intelligence. They also regard you with covetous spirit knowing that I, their would-be killer, am forced to beg of you to give up your life. Great king,' he continued, speaking very softly, as if he told a grave secret, 'do rise. I concede the victory. Rise in triumph and see man, in his defects and shortcomings, kneeling at the gate of your kingdom.'

He was sweating now from something that burnt fiercely inside his chest. In every part of his body there was a great temptation to rest. For the first time he felt the sweet burden of faintness clouding his brain, and fell face down smashing his forehead against the hardness of the ice. Stunned by the heavy blow he lay there motionless, assuming a strange posture of adoration, as if he were paying homage to the elusive kingfish of the creek.

For some seconds he was asleep and dreamed that he was resting on a pile of hay, using the rabbit for a pillow. But soon he woke with violent shivers that shook his whole body. He felt faint again and it worried him.

I must not sleep, he thought. To sleep is death. I must get on my feet and I must move about.

He tied the end of the string to the handle of the pitchfork, then worked his way back to solid ground, crawling on his hands and knees. There he tried to get up, but his legs collapsed under him. He sat down and began to rub the fleshy parts of his legs. Then he tried once again and managed to stand up, swinging backwards and forwards, as the long twigs of willow trees sway in the wind.

Finally he started to move on one way, then the other, with dizzy, wavering steps, being cautious not to lose his balance.

'You could jump now, carp,' he said, 'and I wouldn't have the strength to kill you.'

But, he thought, if you get caught on the hook, the

pitchfork will hold you until I get strong enough to pull you out.

If.

This short word troubled his state of mind. If he became weaker there would be no one to get food for the woman. Without food there is no strength, without strength there is no survival. His friend the blizzard is a ruthless master who favours the strong and kills off the weak. What kind of a provider was he? Was it possible for a real fighter always to lie on the ground? And what about the sea, and his happy life on that sun-baked island? And the banishment of his permanent sadness? Better not ask. Better to do something positive.

He dragged himself wearily, his feet sinking into the soft snow. Once he stumbled and fell but got up again. He was too weak to stand still so he let the wind buffet him.

Suddenly his thoughts took a different direction, and he changed his mind about catching the carp. He made his way towards the cabin which he could clearly see in the fair starlight. The strong breeze pushed him along helpingly, taking the weight off his legs. Treading the path he beat with his own feet three hours ago, he finally reached the cabin.

There he stopped and leaned against the rough timber wall. Shame and horror overwhelmed him because it dawned on him that he would have to kill the rabbit.

For a long time he stood in the half-open door, clutching its wooden frame as if he meant to strangle it. His whole attention was focused on the woman. The dark light of the snow-lit night crawled through the open door and fell upon her sad pale face. He almost waved away the strange beauty of the sight that met his eyes coming through the soft, hazy distance.

She must not die, he thought; she is too young and beautiful. And she carries my little sister within her fatigued body. She must not die.

Still standing in the door, turning his back to the world, he breathed with difficulty. 'She must not die.' Something was repeating this inside him as if to make him learn it by heart.

But someone must die, he realized, and it must be the rabbit. Not because he is unworthy of life, but because he is the smallest among us. And he is also the weakest.

Then he came in, locked the door behind him and lay down upon the dry straw. The solitary nail, in the

83

naked wall, caught his attention and made him think of the fishing line and of the carp. He buried his head in the dry straw and wept freely.

But not for long. Soon he sat up, hastily dried his face, looked around him with tired bitterness and reached for the bottle. He drank the icy melted snow with greedy, long gulps as if he meant to put out the fire that burnt inside his chest. Then he sank back into the soft straw by which he became partly covered and tried to think of nothing.

So he just watched the sooty ceiling and listened to the breeze as it plundered the silent unity of the winter night. He could hear it make swift assaults on the door, squeezing through the long cracks with ill-tempered whisper. Occasionally it softened its temper, and the boy feared that it might die away completely. But it did not. New waves dashed forth recklessly and they brought the fleshy smell of snow with them.

The boy smelled the fresh fragments of the breeze and smiled. My friend the blizzard is not too far off, he thought happily. It has started to descend the high mountains and as it rolls downward it gathers strength and anger. By the time it hits the forest it will have grown into uncontrollable fury, lashing the trees with tall waves of snow, breaking off long branches, hurling them towards the stars. I hope it will kill the carp and I hope it will chase the soldiers down their high towers.

And I hope it will not slay us.

But if it does, it cannot help it. It is its great weight and its foolhardy speed that kill. If I had strong wings I could fly with it. But I am made to crawl and should keep out of its way.

How can I?

And in the dark the boy smiled again because he knew that he could not. He would have liked to send a message to his friend the blizzard perhaps through the puny breeze, that their meeting was inevitable. He would have liked to speak of a power that could not be other than it was; of an urge that made certain actions obligatory. He would have liked to tell him of the sweet freedom of the sea, of the great weight of his sadness and of the happy life on the sun-baked island.

And of the rabbit, too.

But will the blizzard hear his message? He questioned himself. It will not and it cannot. Mighty men can be accused of having deaf ears, for they are born without compassion and live on the sacrifices the meek offer to them. The blizzard is but a part of nature, just as the creek, the forest and the stars are parts of it.

He got up and tiptoed to the woman. She slept soundly, but the rabbit watched him attentively. The boy took him.

'Little brother,' he whispered to the rabbit after he lay down again, 'don't look at me, just listen to what I have to say.'

The rabbit was shivering from fear and tried desperately to break loose.

I cannot fool him, the boy thought sadly. Something, which man calls instinct, tells him my true intention.

'How old are you?' he asked the rabbit. 'Are you as old as the carp? Or is this your first winter?'

The rabbit pulled one side of his face with a sudden jerk as if he meant to smile at the boy.

'You look nice.' The boy smiled back at him. 'And I hope this is not your first winter.'

I'd hate to think that you have never seen spring, he thought. Nevertheless, this can easily be your first winter, and in that case I must tell you about the joys of the spring before I kill you.

But he chose not to speak aloud. He preferred to
86

think, hoping that the rabbit would receive his thoughts. So he thought of the warm breeze that comes from the south in early March. He thought of it so strongly that he could nearly smell the sweet, humid smell of the breeze that filled everyone's lungs with heavy happiness. Then he could see the white brilliance of the snow turn dirty grey and saw it collapse and sink as the flesh sinks on a dead man's face. Then he heard water drop, then flow and then rush from the roofs of houses, from the thick trunks of trees and in the gutters at the sides of the streets. And then there was no more water, and the whole world smelled of the beefy odour which the soft soil gave up. Soon he could perceive innumerable buds, sprouting forth in evergreen swellings, spread over branches and twigs and even on old barks cracked by age. The sun sat firmly established in the sky and it was not the sun which the wintry nature was used to. It was a life-giving ball of fire.

'Yes, little brother,' he whispered, 'such is spring.'

Then he began to pity the rabbit.

'I should never have found you,' he said. 'Or I should have left you there where I found you. But I could not help bringing you here. You see, I have always wanted a pet. Any pet.'

The rabbit looked at the boy as he spoke. With his delicate hind legs he thumped the boy's chest and wetted his coarse shirt.

'Steady, little one,' the boy told him gently. 'It's useless to fight. We are all prisoners and we cannot even help it. It is true that we often dream of freedom. But they are but dreams, little one, just dreams. Even my friend the blizzard is a prisoner.'

I wish I could explain these things to the rabbit, he thought. But I have no time. I must kill him and kill him I must, quickly.

'Saint Anthony,' he said lifting his eyes towards the dark ceiling, 'help me kill the rabbit. You failed me at the creek, don't let me down now. Put the rabbit to sleep and give me the strength to kill him.'

The rabbit gave up the struggle and settled comfortably against the boy's chin. The boy could clearly feel on his Adam's apple the rapid beats of its small heart.

'Bless you, Saint Anthony, for he is going to sleep.'

But after some time the rabbit was still awake, and the boy could see his long ears moving forwards and backwards as if they meant to send him a message coded in mysterious symbols which he could not decipher.

88

'What do you wish to say, little one?' he whispered gently.

Perhaps he remembers the promises I made to him, the boy thought alarmed. Perhaps he remembers the friendship, the protection and the grey flesh of the carp I was talking of.

'Saint Anthony,' he prayed again, 'I'll give the poor my first wages I earn on the English ship, provided you put the rabbit to sleep. People say you are the friend of the poor and of the hopeless. They also say that you are a shrewd one who expects to be paid in advance. But what can I give you? I have only the pocket-knife I must butcher the rabbit with, and the exercise book which truly belongs to my Mama. I can't give the book away, but I shall present the knife to the first poor man I meet. Perhaps I'll cut out the big red star which adorns the cover of the book and give that to him too, although I do not think it would really make anyone happy.'

The rabbit listened carefully to the conversation that went on between his captor and the invisible saint. Then he made a couple of desperate kicks with his hind legs and wetted the boy's shirt for the second time.

'Poor little brother,' the boy spoke to him, 'you

89

must still be a child because you behave like one. I used to wet my bed when I was younger and had bad dreams. Believe me, my Mama was not angry about it. She just shook her head sadly and washed the sheet. Sometimes, on rainy days, we had to sleep on the coarse mattress because the linen had not become thoroughly dry. You see, little one, we only had one bed-sheet.'

Then silence fell between them. The boy found it hard to think of anything. He welcomed the familiar noise of the breeze that steadily increased in strength and tried to push the door in.

'It is my friend the blizzard who makes me kill you,' he spoke out again. 'He speaks with a great howling wail and has no ears for reason. He is powerful and tolerates strong men only. The weak he kills. You know the disadvantage of being weak and small, little one. You understand. I am weak too. So is the woman who must eat for two. One weak one must feed on another in order to be able to stand up against the stronger. Don't ask me who made this injustice the pivot of life. I know as much as you do, though I am able to say what I know. You can't speak, yet you may know just as much as those who can talk loudly about their ignorance.'

Now the boy took some berries out of his pocket and fed them to the rabbit. First the rabbit sniffed at them, then he began to eat one, pushing the others out of the boy's outstretched hand. The boy let them drop in the straw.

No one will need them any more, he thought. They were meant to catch the carp, but the carp had more brains than the rabbit and I. If the rabbit had more sense he would have run away when he first saw me. If I had more brains I would have got more food from the fat man. But the rabbit wanted my friendship and I wanted that of the woman. So we shall lose: the rabbit his life, I my self-esteem. Yet the woman will gain strength and she will bring a new life into this world.

Who can understand these things, he pondered. No one really. If a new life demands the death of an old one, who are the babes that replace the people who hung on the slim Danube bridge? Are they still in their mothers' wombs or are they to be born some time in the future? If so, would they know of the swinging bodies that purchased life for them? Probably not. The Danube carried their corpses down to the Black Sea, or perhaps cast them ashore at the great bend where she turns east to join the

Tisza. And the bridge is swept clean since then. Trams, buses and cars run across it with rumbling noise, and the people seldom look up at the great lamp-posts.

Good for the people that they can forget, the boy thought. I am different. When I shut my eyes I can always see the swinging forest of men and the soldiers who worked among them with silent efficiency, talking in a foreign tongue and occasionally spitting on the pavement.

And the boy closed his eyes. Before he knew it he was asleep.

In his dream he walked on the footpath that led across the bridge. He had no fear in his heart and whistled bravely. The men were all dead and the boy drew his hands gently over the muddy surface of their boots that were tied together with short leather straps. Then he looked up at their faces that were bent downward and had the motionless expression of permanent peace. Then he realized that though the soldiers were gone, there was someone else on the bridge besides him and the dead. She came towards him with slow, unsteady steps. For a moment he thought that she would be his Mama and felt a great happiness overwhelm his chest. But when she came

92

nearer he saw that it was the woman holding his
little sister in her arms. Shock and distress overtook
the boy, because his little sister was naked, covered
with blood. The umbilical cord was still attached to
the centre of her little abdomen and it dangled in the
wind, swinging loosely, with the swaying rhythm of
the muddy boots. The boy started to weep loudly,
and the bridge, the buildings on both sides of the
river, the air and the clouds floating in it, echoed
back his cries a hundredfold.

He came out of sleep and found himself lying on
his face. Something was strongly pressing against his
chest and he realized that it was the rabbit.

Bless your venerable name, Saint Anthony, he
thought relieved. I smothered the rabbit while
I was asleep. He is dead. Now I do not have to
kill him.

He sat up and took the rabbit in his hands.

It was alive.

Well, it must be done, he thought. I hoped I did
not have to kill him. I hoped so much. But what can
I do? The carp let me down and so did Saint
Anthony. What can a man do alone? Do what he
must do. Kill if he has to.

He stood up and went out carrying the rabbit by

his long ears. The cold air bounced upon him like a bird of prey. It penetrated his nostrils and thrust up to his brain.

'Split it,' the boy murmured. 'Split it in two halves, if you want to. One brain was not much of a help. Two halves may serve me better.'

His thin legs trembled with great weakness and his whole body shuddered involuntarily. How does one kill a friend one loves? he asked himself as he leaned against the rough timber wall holding the rabbit by his ears. Does one offer an apology? I do not know. Perhaps, one should make an excuse. But what would it matter? Nothing.

He put the rabbit down and hoped that it would run away. The rabbit crawled back to the boy's feet, trying to shield himself from the strong breeze.

'What do you seek, little one?' the boy asked him gently.

Protection, he thought, that I promised you. But you won't find it here. You will never find it at a man's feet. Man has treachery in his heart and he cannot help it.

Yes, you won't find it, he thought as he lifted up the rabbit from the deep snow. You'll find death. You'll feel your warm blood leak out slowly, painting the virgin white snow crimson. Then the chillness of death will embrace you, and my face will be the last thing you see.

My face, the boy thought sadly. How will it look? Only the rabbit will know and he'll take his secret with him. How did the soldiers' faces look? He tried to remember. They looked neither sad nor angry. They looked busy and professional. But they hanged their enemies. I shall kill a friend.

Oh, Lord, he sighed again, how does a man kill a friend?

But no answer came to him and the boy knew why. I have been living alone for too long, he said to himself. It is hard to live without the presence or aid of a friend, and I have always lived, toiled and had fear alone. The blizzard is my only friend for which I have been waiting for so long. But tomorrow, when it comes, it will want to kill me, not knowing that I am its friend.

Perhaps, the boy thought, that is the secret of smooth killing. Perhaps that is why in war people kill each other without much fuss. They just don't know whom they are shooting at.

But I know the rabbit and he also knows me well. I introduced him to the woman and talked to him of

95

my little sister who lives in the woman's body. I also talked to him of the sea, of the English and of that island where there is warm sunshine all the time.

And I talked to him of a happy life.

'Oh, Christ,' he cried out aloud, 'how does a man kill a friend?'

His cry glided swiftly along the starlit sea of snow and was given back twofold by the solid wall of the pine forest. Yet the boy did not acknowledge its return, for he was treading busily towards the creek. In his mind he saw the long-handled pitchfork lying across the square hole with the string attached to it.

'I am more tired than I ever was,' he murmured to himself, 'but I must see the hook again. If I find the carp dangling on its sharp point, the rabbit will be saved. If not, I shall kill him on the spot.'

But I will not pray again, he thought. I have used up too much time for prayers. I should have known better than to have asked persons who never listen. Prayer is for women who fill the churches on Sundays. Men stay away from church and get drunk. Men know what is good for them and waste no time on idle things.

Yet I should want to speak to Mama. Not to pray,

96

just to talk to her. She promised that she would watch over me day and night. In daytime she just watches, but at night she comes to read the little exercise book. It is now night and I have the book tucked under my shirt. So she must be near.

And the boy looked up at the stars and said wearily:

'Mama, look at the rabbit. And if you are not very far away from God, please go there and see Him on the rabbit's behalf. Not on my behalf, Mama. He does not love me, but perhaps He might like the rabbit.'

Now he paused and listened to the squeaking of the snow under his oversize boots. Then he started to sob and opened his mouth trying to catch his breath.

'Don't look now, Mama,' he whispered gasping for air. 'Just don't look now.'

But soon he composed himself and wiped the tears off his face. Words escaped him and he could not think of anything more to say. So he just moved on, shielding the rabbit from the cold air under his coat. The creek was not far off and he could clearly see the dark contours of the pitchfork.

The hole must have become covered with ice by now, he thought.

It had.

D   97

The boy took his coat off and wrapped the rabbit in it.

'Stay here, little brother,' he spoke to him gently. 'Stay here and wait.'

Then he went down on his hands and knees once again and began to crawl towards the pitchfork. Occasionally he turned his head back, glancing rapidly over his shoulder, to see what the rabbit was doing. He was still there, and the boy could catch a faint glimpse of his long ears that stuck out from under the coat.

The hole was covered by a thin layer of ice, so thin that the boy could easily break it through with his clenched fist. It was a narrow breach he made, just big enough to pull the carp's rocket-shaped body through it.

'I shall have no luck,' the boy said, 'but I still try.'

He started to pull up the string, but stopped half-way. There was no weight on the line.

'Don't be silly,' he spoke to himself sternly. 'Go on. Don't fool yourself and don't attempt to bribe luck. You either have it or you do not have it at all.'

So he pulled up the whole length of the line and looked at the little red berries that neatly covered the

98

point and the shank of the hook. They looked like the red pearls on Mama's rosary beads. The boy remembered Saint Anthony and the prayers he said in vain and threw the fishing line away.

Then with a true anger in his heart he turned about and straightened up. His right hand found the knife in his pocket. Holding it firmly, with the blade bared in the starlight, he made his way back to the rabbit.

There he grabbed the coat and flung it far with great force and suddenness. With his left hand he pressed the rabbit against the frozen earth, with his right he thrust the blade between the shoulders at the base of the neck. Then he covered his face with both of his hands and started to count aloud.

'One ... two ... three ... four ... five ... ' Now he paused and listened to the noise with which the rabbit thumped his life away against the hard clods that were hidden under the soft blanket of snow.

'Six ... seven ... eight ... nine ... ' And he stopped again and bit his lower lip so strongly that it slit open under the pressure and began to bleed freely.

'Ten ... ' he said finally and opened his eyes.

The rabbit lay at the end of a short trail printed with blood in an irregular line. Just then, life visited him for the last time and ran through his small body with quick, nervous shiverings. The boy felt faint, bent forward and vomited. He belched forth water and blood.

'Why do I bleed?' he puzzled over the meagre contents of his stomach. For some time he swayed from side to side, unable to balance the growing weight of his weakness. Seeking solace from his old friends, the stars, he looked up at them. But the great depth of their distance made him dizzier. It was then he realized the advanced state of his sickness.

'The carp ... ' he mused to himself glancing over his back towards the creek. 'The carp is the one that tried to kill me, not the cold night, nor the water that froze over my legs.'

He crawled on his knees to reach the rabbit. The knife slid out smoothly, and the boy wiped it on his trousers. Then he lifted the carcass of the rabbit, and stood up.

A double monologue went on in his mind as he walked his way back to the cabin. The one was cool and businesslike, the other, addressed to the rabbit, soft and compassionate.

'You weigh much less, little brother,' he said. 'You lost your blood and lost your life. Which one was heavier? Perhaps your life. I have lost some blood myself and do not feel lighter.'

Then he looked over the forest and saw rounded masses of thick, white clouds piled up on each other.

'Clear up, head, clear up and think,' he said and hit his forehead with his free hand. 'You should rejoice, for my friend the blizzard is coming and I am well prepared. There is food now, more than I wished for.'

He lifted the carcass and held it at arm's length.

'It will weigh more than four pounds skinned and gutted,' he murmured happily.

His thumb and his first finger ran quickly through the rabbit's fur, feeling the depth of the flesh under it. The legs are well provided for, so is the breast, he thought, and there is meat next to the back bone down to the hind legs.

'I am glad you are so fat,' he said watching the dense steam rising out of his mouth. 'It proves you were not a child. It proves that you had seen many springs. Perhaps, when you went down to the creek for a drink, you had seen the carp, too, cruising deep down. And you probably envied its protection and its great cunning, not knowing that they were your would-be killers.'

Then, in his troubled mind, he attempted to whistle, to prove his boldness and to give himself confidence for the immediate future. But his lower lip was still oozing forth blood, and the sound of his hot breath became buried in the soft, red moisture.

Suddenly sadness overcame him again and made him remember his last dream in the cabin. Nothing is stable in this world, not even the stars, he thought. Everything sways back and forth: the muddy boots of the hanged; the cord that connects my little sister to the woman; my heavy head and the carcass that was the rabbit.

'Little brother,' he said humbly, 'I am sorry that I killed you.'

That was all he could think of. Watching his big shoes sink in the snow he walked with steady rhythm. One day, he thought, I shall throw them away and walk the deck of the English ship barefooted. 'One day—' he said, weighing in his mind the meaning of the word. 'Life is made up of days, and to see tomorrow we must survive today. And I am truly worried about today.'

The thick curtain of clouds slowly rose about the forest. It was moving so tediously that the naked eye could not detect its progress. But the boy was not misled. He knew that the mighty arms of his friend the blizzard would soon lash out. Clouds would empty their bellies, belching out heavy columns of snow upon the earth that would moan in its terror. And above all and behind all and in the midst of all, his friend the blizzard would dance its murderous dance, pulling some into its deadly embrace, flinging others aside.

'Whoa,' the boy cried out aloud, as if his thoughts were galloping horses and he meant to stop them. The cabin was a stone's throw away, and the spot was as good as any to gut and skin the rabbit.

So the boy knelt down and placed the carcass on its back, then he made the sign of the Cross on its breast. Why he did that, he did not exactly know. His Mama always used to cross a new loaf of bread before she had cut it. It was a habit that was acquired and had become automatic, though the boy had never owned a full loaf of bread since his Mama died.

Bending forward and breathing laboriously he cut the rabbit from the throat down to the lower edge of the belly. Pushing the backbone upward with one hand, tearing the intestines out with the other, he emptied the abdominal cavity. After cleaning the

103

gaping hole with plenty of snow he put one knee on the hind legs and commenced to skin the rabbit, cutting long strips of furry skin lengthwise.

When it was all done, and the rabbit lay in the snow naked, lacking the customary covering, a slim bundle of flesh, muscle and sinew, the boy looked at the wedge-shaped strips of skin that were thrown about at random and wondered whether he had made a mistake by cutting the fur into small pieces.

'It was the only way to do it,' he said stubbornly. There was no time to do a proper job. When your hands are cold, it takes time to skin a rabbit. Time was running out, and the boy knew that he did not have much more of it.

Still, I have done a good job, he thought as he stood up and commenced to walk the few yards to the cabin. In the morning I'll serve the woman breakfast in bed. She must eat the white meat of the breast and one of the hind legs. I'll take the other. The rest we'll put in the woman's bag, for we might need it in case we get lost in my friend the blizzard.

Before he opened the door of the cabin, he looked over the scene of his great battle once more. There was a noble satisfaction on his face and he licked his lips contentedly. The coppery, salty taste of his blood reminded him of his slit lower lip and filled him with self-respect.

'I am no longer a boy,' he whispered with true pride. 'Tonight I have proved that I am fit to be a sailor.'

Then he went in and locked the door behind him. He hung the rabbit on the nail, took out the exercise book and rolled it in an armful of straw to make a pillow. In a short time he was asleep.

But that night he did not dream of his Mama, nor of the woman, nor of his little sister, nor of the carp, nor of the blizzard, nor of the bridge. Tonight he dreamed of his island where he walked alone on the hot, sandy beach and watched the roaring surf abate and flow back towards the ocean with the ebb tide. The beach was littered with rubbery brown seaweed and with thousands of different kinds of shells. Some were flat, made up of two halves, joined together at one point by a strong hinge; others were made of one piece and had unusual forms, like the hollow-tooth shells which looked like elephant's tusks. Then, among clumps of weeds, there were broken skeletons of reef-building corals and they were empty and bleached white, but some of them, such as the red, limy organ-pipe coral, remained beautiful even when dead. The boy bent down and picked them up to use them for making necklaces.

Then he went on to the slippery rocks, which were bared by the receding tide, to look for crabs and large, greenish lobsters. Soon he found one that lay in wait under the abrupt edge of a flat rock, but ventured not to touch it because it looked dangerous and hideously ugly as it watched him with its compound eyes, waving its large pincers in the air. So the boy just stepped over the wet monster and climbed up on to the flat rock and lay down on it, stretching his gaunt body to its full length. Strangely, he could see his own body with arms extended in the form of a cross. It looked like a sinewy, ancient gibbet upon which the renegade particles of the breaking waves were thrown and left to die. The colour of the sea around him captivated his attention and he watched breathlessly as it constantly changed from light blue to deep violet. There was no limitation to the range of his vision. Everywhere he cared to look, boundless distance, extending beyond measure, swallowed up his hungry gaze. The world made him know what it really was: an inexhaustible, vast beauty, an endless wonder, an infinite puzzle.

Someone's hand touched his forehead, and the boy

knew it was time to rise, but he would have liked to stay in his dream, so he went on dreaming to see more of the great beauty of the sea.

Yet, after a long look at the rolling surf, he woke and saw the woman's bulky body towering above him.

'How do you feel, little boy?' the woman asked him, and sat down on the pile of straw that was squeezed out of its shape by the boy's resting body.

'I was far away,' the boy answered simply.

'You are sick, little boy.'

'I am happy. I've seen the Island.'

'You have fever.'

'And I have seen the sea making love with the edge of the sky and with great rocks that hide small, brown crabs and large lobsters beneath them.'

The woman blushed and got up from the floor.

'You must eat,' she said sternly as she came back.

The boy saw the roasted rabbit in her hand.

'How did you cook it?'

'It does not matter. I cooked it and you shall eat it.'

'Perhaps I'll eat one of the legs,' the boy said quietly and reached for his knife.

He gave it to the woman because he felt very weak and knew he could not cut the rabbit properly.

The woman sliced the thick, soft meat off the back, but the boy refused to take it.

'It is for you and for the baby girl who lives in your body,' he said in a strong voice.

The woman reddened in the cheeks again.

'What makes you think it will be a girl?'

'I just know,' the boy said quietly. 'Didn't I guess the rabbit's sex rightly?'

'I don't know. Did you?'

The boy paused in silence, looking out of the small window, then said:

'I did. He was a male. He did not run away.'

'I see ... ' the woman said calmly.

They ate in silence. Outside, though it was past noon, there reigned semi-darkness because of the heavy, grey clouds that overtook the whole sky. The boy felt his heart in his throat and could hardly swallow the juicy flesh of the rabbit.

My friend the blizzard will soon be here, he thought, and I am as weak as a newly born babe. He chewed every small bit thoroughly. Perhaps it was not too late. Perhaps he could still gain strength.

The same problem troubled the woman's mind, too.

'A blizzard is coming,' she said after some hesitation.

'I know. It is my friend.'

'Your friend?' the woman asked, puzzled.

'Yes. And yours, too.'

He is delirious, the woman thought, and I must get him help as soon as it is practicable.

'The blizzard is a cruel killer, little boy.'

'It is strong, not cruel.'

'Have it your own way.' The woman smiled faintly. 'Nevertheless, we must get away from here.'

'We shall as soon as it arrives.'

You just eat now, little boy, the woman thought sadly, then you just fall asleep. And while you are dreaming of your island in the sea I'll get back here with a doctor. We shall go east, little boy, not west. Life should be preserved, not wasted. You do not yet know much about these things and probably will never grasp them, for you are a male, lovable and foolhardy. But if you felt the life that kicks wildly against the wall of my swollen stomach you would understand why I am going to betray you. Of course, you will hate me for it. I shall understand. You are a man, therefore you prefer to die rather than to turn back. I know, yet I will still cheat you. It is easy to die, little boy. It is, sometimes, more comfortable to throw life away than to bear it. *But*, and you will never be able to understand this because you are a male, lovable and foolhardy; it is more than hard, more than beautiful, more than sacred to carry a new life in one's body and help it to get out.

Then the woman laid the remains of the rabbit on the window shelf and looked down at the boy who was fast asleep.

'One day,' she whispered gently, 'you'll go west, little boy, or perhaps the west will come for you. One day you may sail upon the seven seas freely and proudly and I hope that on that day you will forgive me.'

She knelt, because it was impossible for her to bend down to kiss the boy.

'But now,' she said with true sadness in her voice, 'I shall betray you.'

She got up from the floor, and with long, heavy steps walked out of the cabin.

One hour later a crashing sound roused the boy from sleep. The wind broke the window-pane, hurtling broken pieces of glass all over the room. Then the angry current of air threw the door wide open, banging it against the creaking door post. The thousands of hollow stalks of straw jumped high in the air and whirled through the door spinning swiftly around in an insane orbit. The boy grabbed

112

the little exercise book and, holding it with his left hand, crawled to the wall. There he stooped low, his limbs drawn close to his body, and watched with amazement as the inrush of cold air filled the empty cabin with snow, frozen leaves and broken, dry twigs.

'This is it,' he finally managed to whisper. 'This is what I have been waiting for. It blows from the east and it blows hard. Now I do not have to walk against it. I can sail with it. In no time I'll be on the edge of the forest.'

He started to move towards the corner where his blanket was laid, creeping quietly and with great caution as if he tried to avoid being seen.

Just then he remembered the woman.

'Where is she?' he shouted in a loud voice, and sat down, leaning against the timber wall. The force of

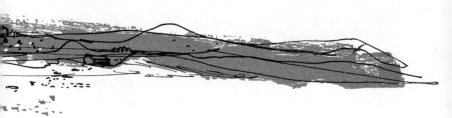

the wind chilled his back as it squeezed the cold air through the minute cracks between the long logs.

The boy reached out for the blanket and threw it around his shoulders. Where is she? And he tried to remember their last conversation. Yes. She wanted to get away before the blizzard arrived.

He did not say: my friend the blizzard. Now that his great friend was really present, bellowing above the cabin with rumbling roar, proclaiming loudly its omnipotence above things dead or alive, shaking the huge, pregnant clouds with heavy hands, throwing columns of snow up in the air with frightful ease, the boy did not like to offend the blizzard by calling it his friend.

'Yes,' he murmured to himself, 'she wanted to get away.' But where to? He tried to puzzle it out. And why without me? And when? Before or after the blizzard had arrived?

She could not have gone back. Nobody would want to go back. Everyone wants to go away. Therefore she must have gone west, and now she is tumbling towards the forest, with hurried, awkward steps, watching the thick, falling branches, praying for the safety of my little sister.

But why without me?

Because she slept all the way through the night and did not witness the great battle I fought to get the carp. Now she thinks I am a mere boy, sick and enfeebled, as weak as the rabbit I killed. Women like the protection of big men who are raw and strong and so healthy that they can curse God with laughter.

'But I forgive and I understand,' he spoke with great peace in his heart. 'I understand,' he said again and somewhat louder as if he meant to explain this to his blatant friend the blizzard. Above all things, the woman must think of my little sister and because of my little sister she must fight everyone. She must betray a friend. She must even cheat herself. It may be true that when she is dreaming she hates my little sister, but when she is awake she walks about with a sad smile and loves the cruel weight that pulls her heart down towards the frozen soil.

'Of course, wind,' he whispered bitterly between his clenched teeth as he watched the insane fury of his friend the blizzard streaming through the window, sweeping the rabbit's mutilated carcass along the dirt floor towards the open door. 'You will never understand these things. Not because you are an impersonal thing, but because you are too strong.

The strong is the prisoner of his own strength. Not so the fat man who is weak and therefore can do what he does not wish to do. You must do what you ought to do because you are a giant and everyone sees you.'

'It is also true,' the boy added nodding approvingly, 'that you die too. But you kill many before you go.'

Then he stood up, wrapped the blanket about his gaunt figure and started to walk to the door. The constant surge of the wind caught him in the middle of the cabin and hurled him through the door. Outside, it spun him round on his heel in a whirl of snow, pushed him down to the earth and dropped the carcass of the rabbit on his chest.

'There is much more wind in the blizzard than we thought, little brother.' He would have liked to say something more to the rabbit, but it was blown off his chest. For a moment the boy could see it floating in the air, then it dropped out of sight.

So he just lay quietly for a long while and thought of what the woman would say to him in the forest. There was no doubt in his mind. He would catch up with her before the edge of the forest, but he knew he would not rebuke her for her little faith.

I forgive and I understand. That's all. We shall never talk about this. Not even on the Island.

Using all his strength he dragged himself up, but the blizzard knocked him down again.

I should have grabbed the rabbit while it was lying on my chest, he thought, and should have eaten some more of it. But I am still drowsy with sleepiness. That's why I keep doing things wrongly.

Only his head was out of the snow; the rest of him was covered by it. Strangely, he was warm and comfortable. How simple it would be if he only could command nature. What order should he give it now? With every iota of his whole being he willed:

Be still!

As if in answer to his wish, a rolling wave of snow closed fast behind and with a dull roar hit him. He thought he had been buried alive and was afraid to move for a moment. But then he stood up and found himself erect, protected by a thick pile of snow that took the form of a great cone, the boy's head being its apex.

It will soon be blown away, the boy reassured himself. In the meantime I must have a rest and give my legs a chance to get used to the weight of my body.

But before he could gather more confidence under the windproof mantle of snow, the blizzard had torn it away from him.

'You did not let me keep it for long,' he said in a friendly manner.

There was no enmity in him. He did not do so badly. Not as yet, anyhow. Though he stumbled and fell he managed to get up again and was moving now, the great hand of the blizzard pushing him towards the forest.

What has happened to the soldiers? he speculated. They must be huddled close together, from fear and for warmth, under their tall towers. For them to-morrow is just another day. For me it is another life.

He kept wrapping himself up in the blanket, and dragged himself stubbornly, his feet sinking in the deep snow and the wind buffeting him.

'It won't be long now,' he mused to give himself endurance. I'll soon meet the English who live on an island and have ships of all sizes. But how shall I talk to them? I'll manage, somehow. I learned a few words of the soldiers' language, although I never really liked them. The English I like, therefore I shall speak their tongue with ease.

He knelt down and rested for what he believed to
118

be ten minutes. It was not so dark now because his friend the blizzard thinned out some of the clouds, tearing half their thickness away from the sky. The boy could fairly see to a distance of about half a kilometre. After a while he became puzzled, looking at a snow-covered object that appeared to be the cabin.

The storm has turned me about and now I am heading back to the place where I set out from, he realized.

He struggled to his feet again and continued to walk, leaning against the current of wind, turning his back to the cabin. His breathing became quite difficult now, and large grey spots danced before his eyes.

I had been seeing things before now, he reassured himself. There is no cause for panic.

But deep within his consciousness his instinct warned him.

'I hope I do not have to rest again,' he mumbled through his partly closed lips.

And he kept on circling in the blinding snow-storm, wet with sweat, chilled to the bone. His throat was dry and he reached for the snow, but could not bend down, so he just opened his mouth and let the blizzard fill it with icy, sharp crystals.

Thrice he passed the cabin during the next hour, and each time he felt himself go.

'I wish this was a bad dream,' he cried aloud. 'But don't wish now. Just walk. And walk straight.'

His friend the blizzard grew stronger as if it meant to show the boundless energy it collected,

rolling unchecked across the Great Hungarian Plain. The boy hunched his back against its wild strength. For a short while he managed to stay on his feet, but then collapsed suddenly and lay listless as though a great hand had fallen upon him.

It is over, he thought. What can I do now? Nothing.

So he just watched the grand drama his friend the blizzard played for him. He watched the snow being churned into restless foam, then into giant whirlpools that spiralled high up and met their dull parents, the clouds, drawing floating objects into their centres which looked like the gaping mouths of insane women. He heard the sharp shrill of the air as it was hopelessly boxed up between heaven and earth and tried to escape its own mounting weight, shrieking with piercing cry in its terror. Then he buried his head in the snow and pressed his ears to the ground and heard it moan in a low and gentle whinny.

'The whole world is suffering,' he whispered in fear mingled with admiration. There was a great temptation to leave his head lying on the soil and doze off, muffled up within the snow.

'Don't be silly,' he reprimanded himself severely. 'Don't be silly and go on. If you can't walk, then crawl.'

He started to move on his hands and knees,

dragging his body along the frozen clods, slowly and painfully, as a worm. His head felt giddy and unsteady and he let it drop and let it dangle between his arms, unable to support it any more. He hoped the blizzard would not turn him in the opposite direction again.

After a while he could see the grim forest marching at cloud level.

It is because I am stooped low, and the clouds are crouched down too, he reasoned. The nearer I get to it the more I see of it. And the more I see of it the safer I feel. Once among its tall trees, I can stand up again and move on faster.

Occasionally he stopped and raised his head to look for the woman. But he did not see her. Perhaps she has reached the forest, he thought, and now she is settled comfortably against the strong trunk of a pine tree and watches my progress.

But she should not sit facing the blizzard. She should think of my little sister and turn her back to the wind. And she should have taken the blanket to wrap it round her bulky stomach.

Then he realized he had lost the blanket.

'Where did I drop it?' he mused to himself and managed a faint smile.

Confidence began to return to him, and the

distance between him and the growing forest seemed to shrink steadily.

And then, something broke in him abruptly and irreparably. He fell face down and a violent spasm made him vomit thick blood. It kept returning in very quick succession and the boy tried to fight it. He turned over, lay on his back and pounded his chest with short, heavy blows.

Two minutes later the convulsion left him.

He commenced to crawl again but was forced to stop immediately.

There was nothing more to do. Just wait. Slowly he turned over again and placed his left arm under his head. With his right hand he searched his coat for the exercise book, but could not find it.

They have beaten me, he thought sadly. Not the soldiers. They can never really beat anyone. They kill people, never defeat them. But my friends, the blizzard and the woman. They have beaten me. The blizzard knew not that I was its friend and the woman went away alone. Together we could have held hands in the snow-storm.

Yes, he thought, it is a great thing to hold someone's hand.

Then he did not want to think of anything any more.

The snow covered his head up, and the boy closed his eyes peacefully under its gentle weight. Soon he was asleep, but he did not dream of persons, nor of the shapes of things. He dreamed of colours: of white, lilac and garnet; of red, gold and blue; of pale yellow and violet; of greyish-green and purple. Then the reflecting rays blended promiscuously

125

into a new colour that he had never seen before.

The boy wanted to see more of this wonder and kept his eyes shut forcefully. But soon small, soiled spots came forth from the four corners of his eyes, growing in size and spreading with great speed.

Yet, before they could absorb the beauty of his dream — the boy had died.

Next morning his friend the blizzard vanished, and two soldiers who were on their way to the village found the boy's body covered half in snow and half in frozen leaves. The younger soldier stepped over the corpse in a hurry because he had a girl waiting for him, but the other, who was a sergeant and much older, called him back.

Together they shouldered the rigid corpse, which was so light that the young soldier decided not to make any complaint.

So they just walked silently and with military precision, being cautious not to drop the body that stretched across the void between their shoulders and looked in the strong rays of the morning sun like a slender ship which had furled its sails and slid into a haven in search of safe anchorage.

126

F
Mar   Marton, Gregory
c.2   The boy and his friend
        the blizzard.